D1049916

I Can Read!™

# Adventures of the JUSTICE LEAGUE™

ADVENTURES OF THE JUSTICE LEAGUE


For information address HarperCollins Children's Books, a division of HarperCollins Publishers,
195 Broadway, New York, NY 10007.
www.icanread.com

ISBN: 978-0-06-244180-5
Manufactured in Dong Guan City, China
Lot#:
15 16 17 18 19 SCP 5 4 3 2 1
08/15

# Adventures of the JUSTICE LEAGUE™

HARPER
*An Imprint of HarperCollinsPublishers*

# TABLE OF CONTENTS

# I Am Wonder Woman

Written by Erin K. Stein
Illustrations by Rick Farley

WONDER WOMAN created by William Moulton Marston

My name is Princess Diana.
I grew up in a secret place
called Paradise Island.
I am an Amazon.

My mother is Queen Hippolyta.
She rules the Amazons
and protects Paradise Island.
All Amazons are strong warriors.

The Greek gods told my mother
about the dangers in the world.
Mankind needed someone
to keep the world safe.

The gods wanted to send the best Amazon warrior to do the job.

The Queen had a contest to see which of us was faster, stronger, and braver than all the others.

Though I was a princess,
I did not want to become queen.
I wanted to fight for justice.
I secretly entered the contest.

I tried my best to win.

All of my arrows hit the target.

I outran all my Amazon sisters.

Our bracelets work as shields.
I moved as fast as lightning
to block all the arrows
fired by my opponents.

In the last sword fight,
I beat all the other finalists.
After I won, I showed my face
to the crowd.

My mother was surprised
but also very proud.
“Diana, you have earned it.
You are a champion,” she said.

She gave me a special costume and a new title to go with it: Wonder Woman.

The Greek gods gave me
the ability to talk to animals
and a magic lasso
that makes people tell the truth.

To keep Paradise Island a secret,
I fly my Invisible Jet
so no one can see where I go.

I left Paradise Island
to live in Washington, DC.
My secret identity
is Diana Prince.

I work for the government
at a top secret agency.
At my job, I find out first
when there is trouble.

Two important reports come in.
An old bridge will collapse
the next time a train goes across.
And there's a crime at the zoo!
I spin very fast to change
into my super hero costume.
I rush to the rescue as Wonder Woman!

I fly through the city
faster than the speed of sound.
I use my super-strength
to help those in danger.

Just as the bridge collapses
I carry the train to safety.

There's no time to rest.

A tiger was stolen from the zoo!

Two strange men start to run.

"Stop!" I shout.

I toss my Lasso of Truth

and catch the robbers.

The lasso makes them tell me

where they hid the tiger.

BENGA
GAL TIGE

Sometimes I have no choice
but to fight an enemy.
My friends Superman and Batman help
me train for all forms of combat.

Not every crime is easy to stop.
I must be prepared for anything,
even mythical beasts!

As Wonder Woman, I am famous.

My secret identity

lets me live a normal life, too.

Only my closest friends

know my secret. . . .

I am Wonder Woman!

# I Am Aquaman

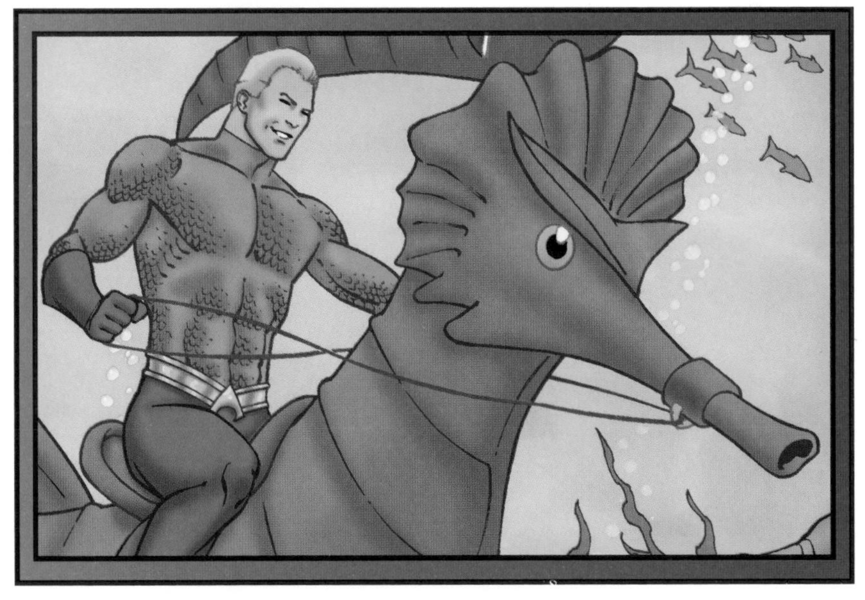

by Kirsten Mayer
pictures by Andy Smith
colors by Brad Vancata

AQUAMAN created by Paul Norris

Under the sea is a land
called Atlantis.
Aquaman and Mera
are king and queen of Atlantis.
Aquaman protects the sea
and also helps humans on land.
He is on a team of super heroes
called the Justice League.

The other heroes are coming
to see Atlantis and meet Mera.
Aquaman greets Green Lantern,
Wonder Woman, Batman, and Superman
on the surface of the water.
"Hello, friends! Welcome to the sea!
I have sea horses for you to ride."
The sea horses poke their heads out.

"I can't wait to meet Mera,"

says Wonder Woman.

"And to see your castle,"

says Superman.

"What sort of power source
do you use under the sea?"
asks Batman.
Aquaman chuckles.
"Come see for yourselves!"

“Here, this will help.”
Green Lantern uses his power ring
to create face masks for the heroes
so they can all go underwater.
Aquaman can breathe underwater
and Superman can hold his breath.
Everyone rides sea horses down
to the bottom of the ocean.
They enter the city of Atlantis.

Aquaman points out Mercy Reef
and the hydropower plant.
The group gets off the sea horses
and swims into a golden castle.

"Here is my throne room,"
Aquaman says.
"Topo, off the chair."
The king shoos his pet octopus.

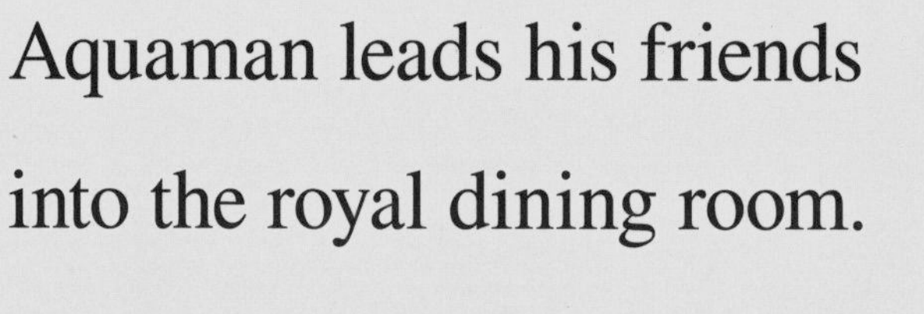

Aquaman leads his friends

into the royal dining room.

It is filled with air, so they can breathe.

Green Lantern waves away their face masks.

"Welcome, everyone," says Mera.
"Arthur has told me so much
about each of you."
They all sit at a large table
covered with lots of delicious food.

Topo swims out to play
with his friends.
A dark shape swoops by.
It is Aquaman's enemy
Black Manta!

In the dining room,
Aquaman drops his fork.
“We are under attack!”
he cries.

“How do you know?”
asks Superman.
“Topo and the dolphins—
I can hear them in my mind,”
says the king.

The heroes jump to their feet.
Wonder Woman says,
"We will help defend your home.
Hal, face masks please."
Green Lantern gives them face masks.
The team jumps into the water
and swims out to face the enemy.

Black Manta arrives.
He swims out of his ship
in his diving suit and helmet.
“I will be king now,”
he says to Aquaman.
“My buddy and his sharks
will take care of your friends.”

Green Lantern uses his ring
to form a big fishing net.
Queen Mera has powers, too.

Mera controls the water currents
and forces the fish toward her friend.
"Catch!" she yells to Green Lantern.
He closes the net around the sharks.

King Shark tries to bite
Superman with his big teeth.
He punches the shark on the nose!

“Here’s the biggest catch of the day!” Superman says to Green Lantern as the shark sails right into the net.

Black Manta fires
laser rays from his helmet.
Wonder Woman deflects the rays
with her silver bracelets.
Aquaman fights back
with his mighty trident.
“I rule Atlantis, Black Manta!”
he commands. “No one else!”

Batman gets into Manta’s ship.
He zooms by and scoops up the foes.
Then Batman jumps out of the ship
and swims to his friends.
Aquaman forms a whirlpool
and sends the scoundrels far away.
The super heroes cheer.
Atlantis is safe once again!

Aquaman says,
"Thanks to all of you,
we showed Black Manta there is
only one King of the Seas.
I am Aquaman!"

# I Am Green Lantern

by Ray Santos
pictures by Steven E. Gordon
colors by Eric A. Gordon

The Green Lantern Corps protects the universe. Each Green Lantern is in charge of a different sector.

Hal Jordan guards Sector 2814.

The planet Earth is in Sector 2814.
It is Hal's job
to make sure no aliens attack Earth
or any other planet in his sector.

Hal wasn't always a Green Lantern. He was once a regular boy who grew up in a town called Coast City.

When he was older,
Hal became a test pilot,
just like his father had been.

It was a dangerous job,

but he wasn't afraid.

Hal wasn't afraid of anything.

Before Hal, Sector 2814's Green Lantern was an alien named Abin Sur.

He had protected the area for a long time.

Abin Sur got into a bad fight,
and his spaceship was damaged.
It was headed on a crash course
with Earth, and he couldn't stop it.

Abin Sur knew that he
wouldn't survive the crash.
A new Green Lantern
had to be found.
He used his Green Lantern
power ring to find someone
who was worthy.

Hal saw Abin Sur's ship crashing to Earth. Something called him to the crash site. He knew that he had to go there. As soon as Hal saw the crashed ship, he ran over to it.

He had never seen a spaceship
or an alien before, but he wasn't scared.

"The ring has chosen you,"
the alien said.
Abin Sur held out his
Green Lantern power ring.
"Because you are a person
who can overcome great fear,"
Abin Sur added.
The ring floated through the air to Hal.

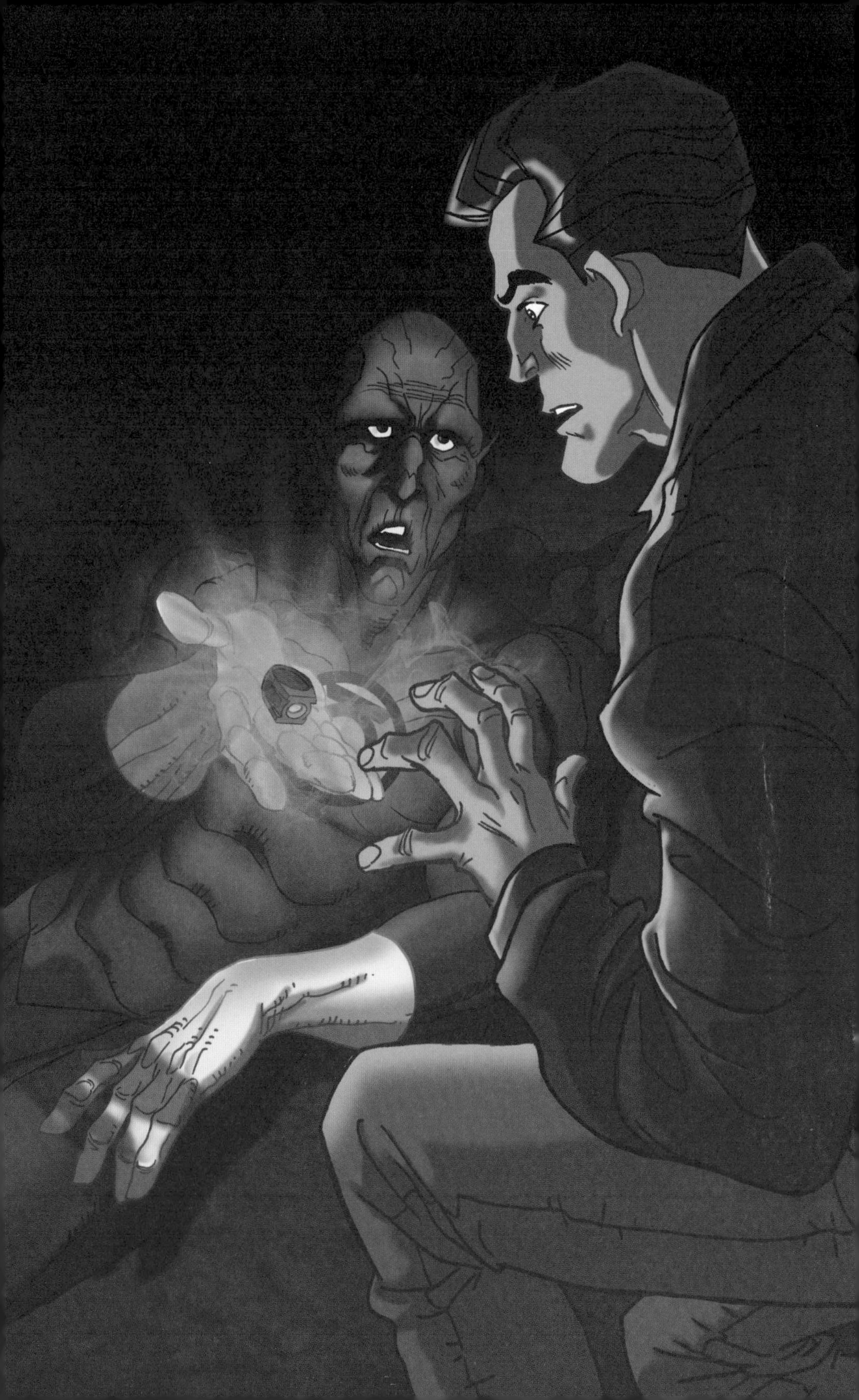

Hal put the ring on his finger,
and his clothes turned into
a Green Lantern uniform.
"Welcome to the Green Lantern Corps,"
Abin Sur said to him.
"Your ring is what gives you
your powers," the alien said.
"Its green energy can form
into anything you can imagine."
He told Hal that fear was the only
thing that could defeat a Green Lantern.

The ring took Hal to the
Green Lantern home world of Oa.

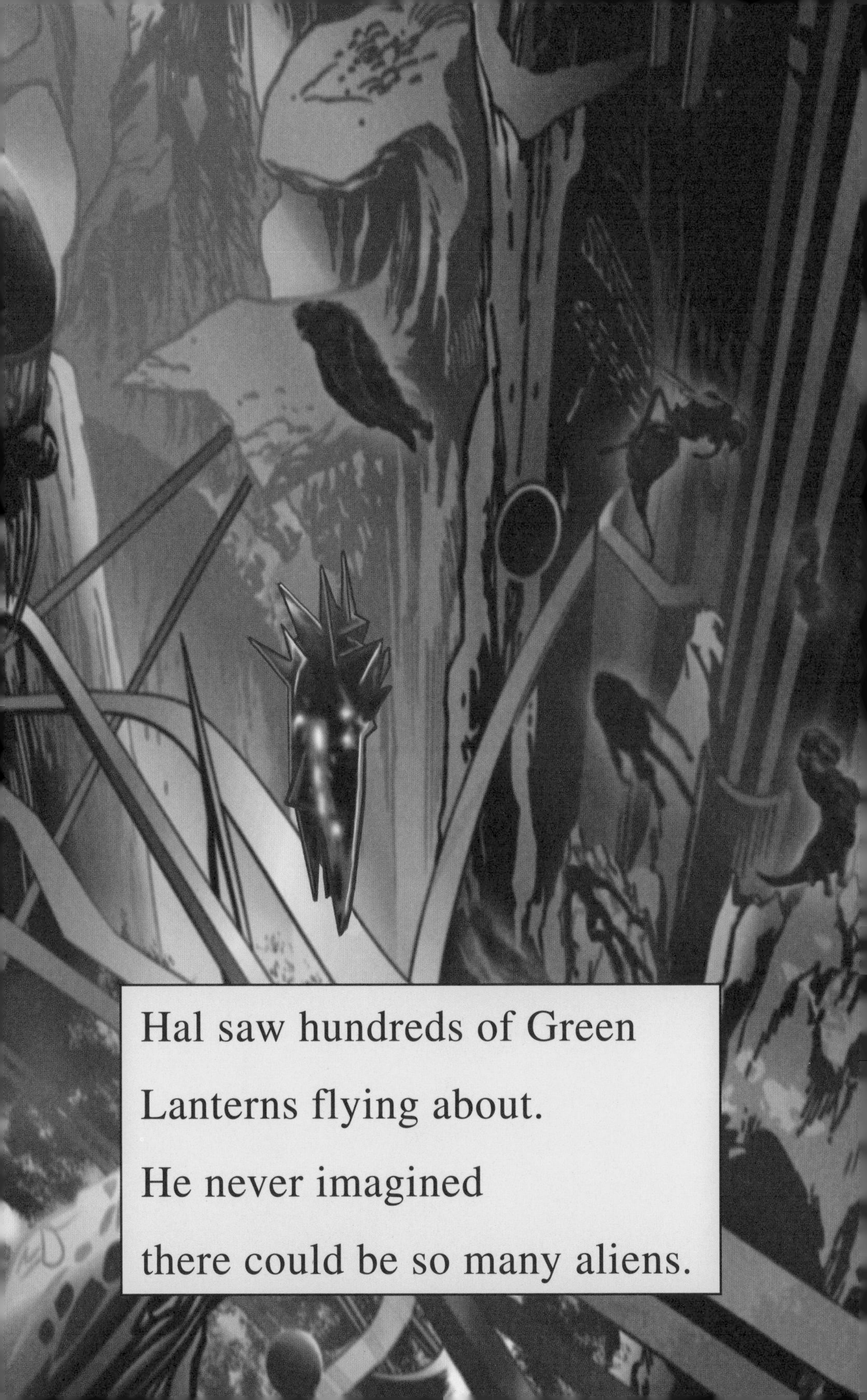
Hal saw hundreds of Green
Lanterns flying about.
He never imagined
there could be so many aliens.

To master his new powers,
Hal trained with a Green Lantern
named Kilowog.

Kilowog was the toughest
of the Green Lanterns.
Hal knew that he couldn't be afraid
of this mean-looking alien.

It wasn't easy, but Hal overcame his fears and finished his training with Kilowog. He became an official member of the Green Lantern Corps.

Using what Kilowog taught him,

Hal returned to Earth as its new protector.

No matter how tough an enemy was,

Hal was never scared.

With his new Green Lantern powers,
Hal joined the Justice League.
As a defender of Earth, he stood
alongside the World's Greatest Super Heroes.

He teamed up with The Flash and Martian Manhunter to battle Sinestro.

Sinestro was a former Green Lantern and was just as strong as Hal.

But he wasn't as strong as the combined power of the Justice League.

Like all great heroes, Hal knew that he was stronger with the help of his friends.

As Hal fought to defend Earth from countless villains, he always heard the Green Lantern oath in his head.

In brightest day, in blackest night,
no evil shall escape my sight.
Let those who worship evil's might
beware my power—Green Lantern's light!

# I Am The Flash

by John Sazaklis
pictures by Steven E. Gordon
colors by Eric A. Gordon

Meet Barry Allen.
He lives in Central City.
He works as a scientist
at the Central City
Police Department.
Barry also has a big secret.

CE
POLI

A few years ago,
Barry was working late
inside the police lab.
Outside, there was a
raging thunderstorm.

Suddenly, a bolt
of lightning crashed
through the window!

Many different chemicals
spilled onto Barry's body.
The special combination
had a strange effect on him.

Barry's legs began to tingle.
Before he knew it,
the young scientist
was running out the door!

Barry ran all the way home
in less than a minute.
The accident had given him
the power of super-speed.
Barry decided to protect
Central City with his new ability.
He created a special suit
to hide his true identity.
Barry became The Flash—
the Fastest Man Alive!

As time went on,

Barry fine-tuned his powers.

He could run up walls!

He could run on water!

Barry could spin his arms so fast that they created whirlwinds.

The crooks and criminals of Central City were no match for this speedy new super hero.

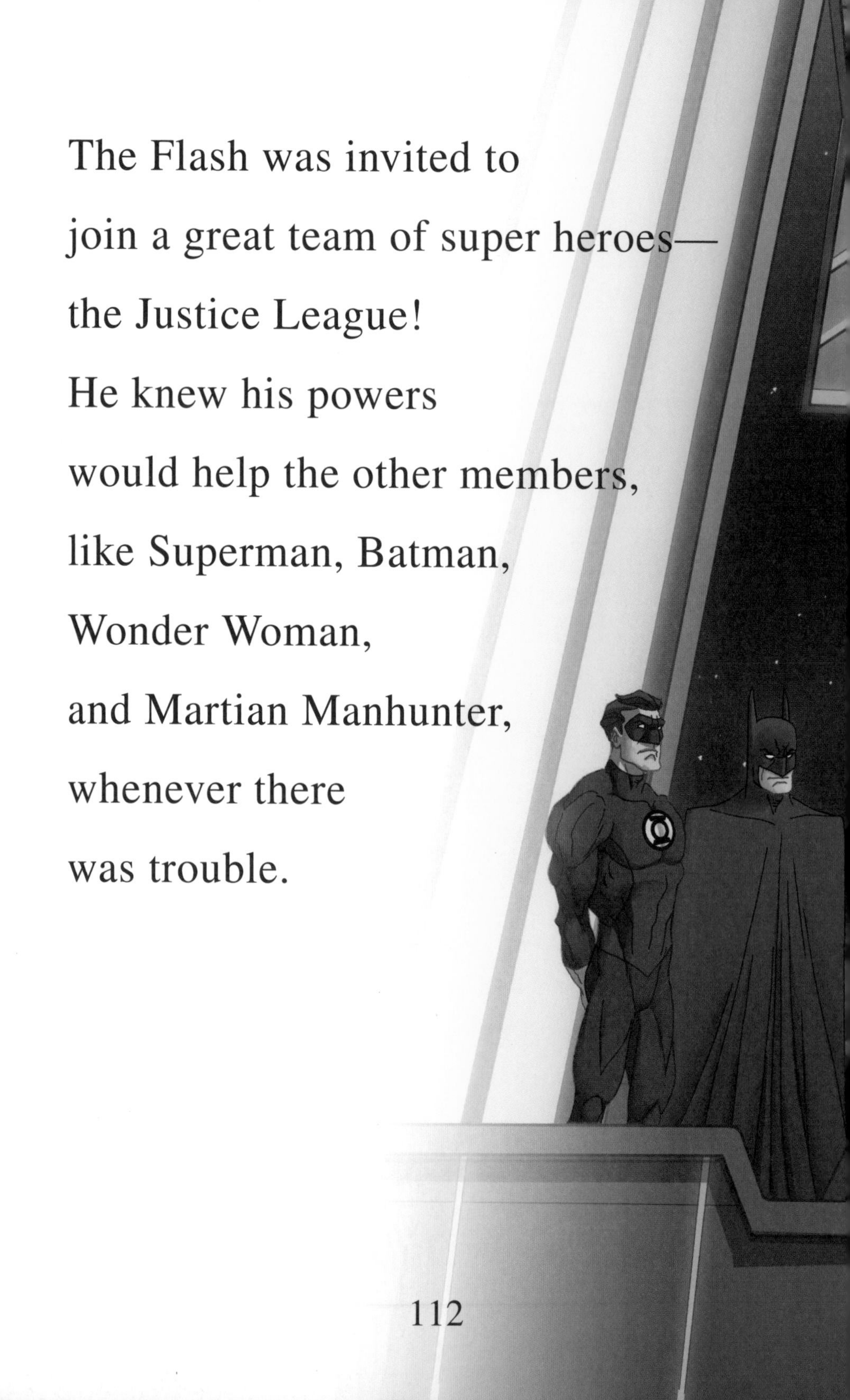

The Flash was invited to
join a great team of super heroes—
the Justice League!
He knew his powers
would help the other members,
like Superman, Batman,
Wonder Woman,
and Martian Manhunter,
whenever there
was trouble.

Barry is working
when he sees a breaking
news report on the television.
All of the super-villains
have broken out of jail!

“It’s time to speed things up,”

Barry says.

In the blink of an eye,

Barry becomes The Flash!

The Flash calls the Justice League.
Then he zooms to the prison.
Ultra-Humanite is behind the escape.
The mad scientist implanted his brain
into the body of a mutant ape,
making himself a fierce enemy.

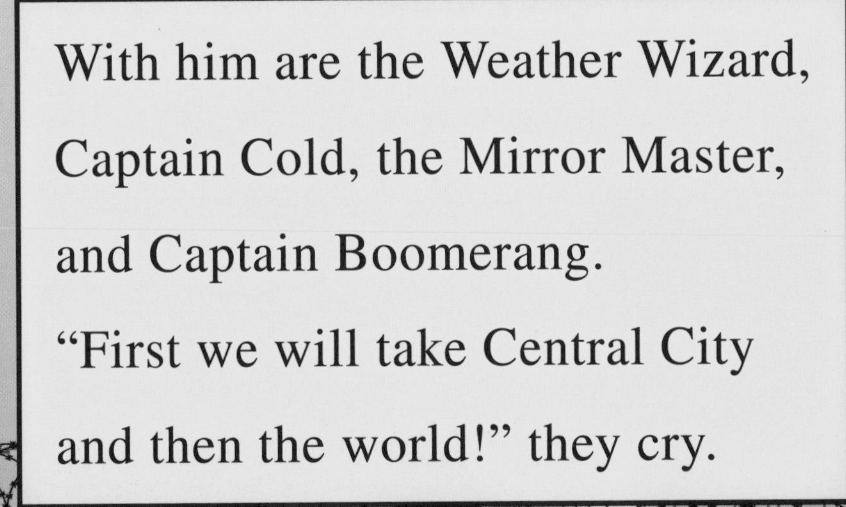

With him are the Weather Wizard,
Captain Cold, the Mirror Master,
and Captain Boomerang.
“First we will take Central City
and then the world!” they cry.

"All you're taking is a trip back to jail," says The Flash. "You cannot fight us alone!" shouts Ultra-Humanite.

“That is why I got a little help
from my friends,” replies The Flash.
The Justice League arrives—
ready for action!

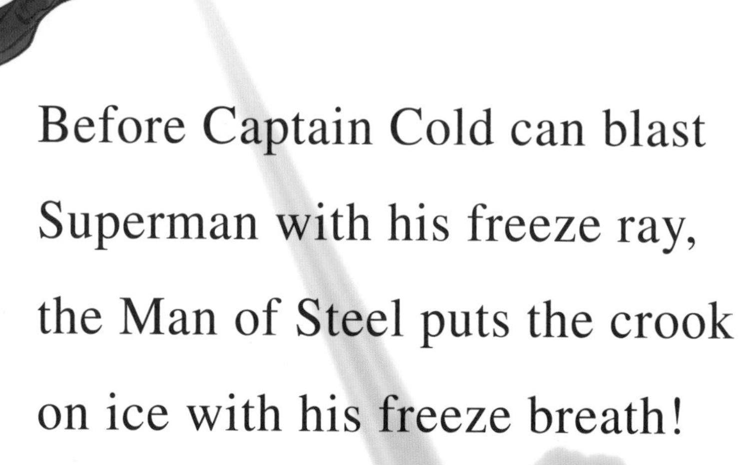

Before Captain Cold can blast
Superman with his freeze ray,
the Man of Steel puts the crook
on ice with his freeze breath!

The Weather Wizard attacks
Batman with his weather wand.
Quickly, the Caped Crusader
knocks him out with a Batarang.

Captain Boomerang is
no match for Wonder Woman.
She ties him up with her
Golden Lasso of Truth.

The Mirror Master uses tricks to try
to fool Martian Manhunter.
The hero uses his mental powers
to take down the crafty crook.

Finally, The Flash goes up
against Ultra-Humanite.
"I will pound you into the ground!"
growls the mutant gorilla.

“Catch me if you can!” says The Flash.
“Keep your eyes on the moving target!”
He zigs and he zags and he zooms
swiftly around Ultra-Humanite.

The Scarlet Speedster zips faster
and faster and faster in a big circle.
The extreme speed creates a tornado
that lifts the villains up into the air.
The strong winds send the criminals
spiraling over the prison wall,
back to where they came from.
"Thanks for your help, my friends,"
The Flash says to the Justice League.
"Central City is safe once again."

"Bad guys had better beware,"

says the hero.

"I am the protector of Central City.

I am the Fastest Man Alive.

I am The Flash!"

# I Am Superman

by Michael Teitelbaum
pictures by Rick Farley

SUPERMAN created by Jerry Siegel and Joe Shuster

## CLARK KENT

Clark Kent is a
newspaper reporter.
He is secretly Superman.

## LOIS LANE

Lois Lane is a reporter.
She works for the
Daily Planet newspaper.

## LEX LUTHOR

Lex Luthor is the
smartest criminal
in the world.
He is Superman's enemy.

## THE FORTRESS OF SOLITUDE

This is Superman's hidden home.
Many secrets about his life are inside.

## SUPERMAN

Superman has many amazing powers.
He was born on the planet Krypton.

Lois Lane sped past Clark Kent.
She was on her way out of
the Daily Planet,
where she and Clark worked.
They were newspaper reporters.

“Why are you in such a hurry, Lois?”

asked Clark.

“I’m writing a story,” Lois said.

“What kind of story?” Clark asked.

“That’s my secret!” Lois said.

Lois rushed up to the roof.

Superman was waiting for her there.

“Hi, Lois,” Superman said.

“Ready to do the story?”

“You bet, Superman!” Lois said.

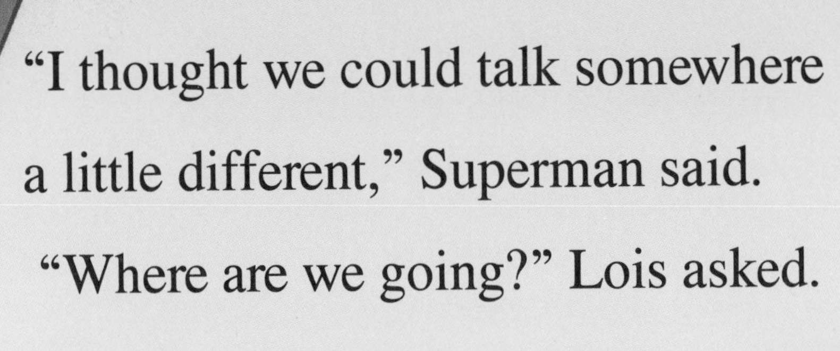

"I thought we could talk somewhere a little different," Superman said.

"Where are we going?" Lois asked.

"You'll see," said Superman.

Superman flew at super-speed
up to the frozen Arctic.
“This is my Fortress of Solitude,”
Superman said.

“The Fortress is my secret home,”
he told Lois.
“If you want to learn about me,
this is the best place to come.”

“This giant key unlocks the door,”

Superman said.

He put the key into the lock.

“I use my super-strength to lift it.”

Superman and Lois
entered the Fortress.
Superman used his super-breath
to blow the door closed.
"That's amazing!" said Lois.

Lois pointed at two statues.

“Who are those people?” she asked.

“Those are my parents,”

Superman said.

“My father, Jor-El,

and my mother, Lara.

They’re holding a model of Krypton.”

“Krypton?” Lois asked.

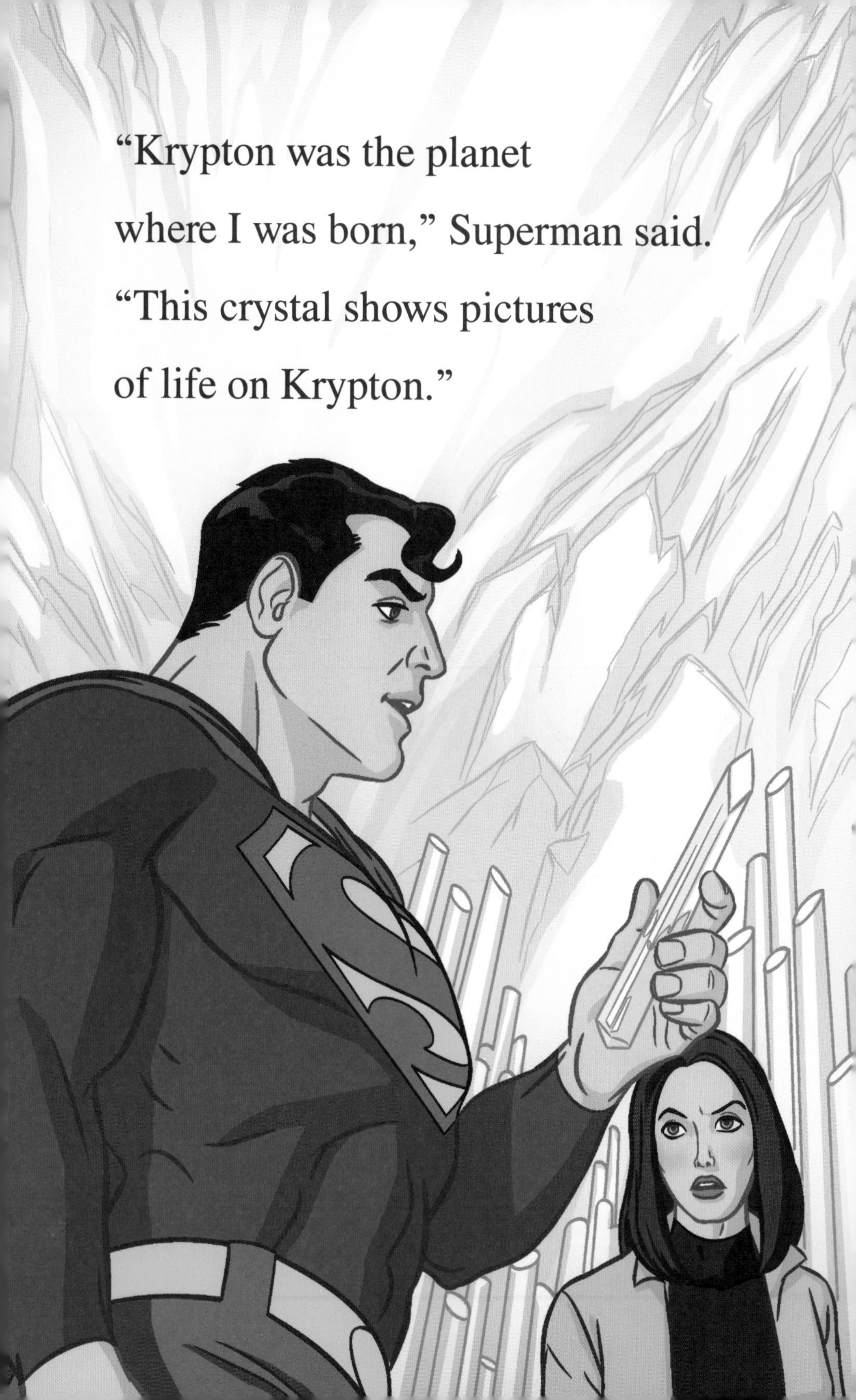

"Krypton was the planet
where I was born," Superman said.
"This crystal shows pictures
of life on Krypton."

“Krypton was different from Earth, but it was my home,” said Superman. “Then one day my father learned that Krypton was going to explode.”

"My father put me in a spaceship
and sent it to Earth
to save my life," Superman said.

“Earth’s yellow sun gives me
my superpowers,” said Superman.
“Even when I was a little boy,
I could lift a truck.”

"Wow," said Lois.

"What else can you do?"

"I can see through things

with my X-ray vision," Superman said.

"And nothing can hurt me."

"Nothing?" Lois asked.

"Only kryptonite can make me weak,"

Superman said.

"It's a piece of my home planet.

I keep it in this case so it can't hurt me."

Suddenly, an alarm rang out.
Lex Luthor's angry face
filled up the computer screen.
"I will rule the city!" said Luthor.
"Watch what will happen
if I'm not given complete power!"

“Metropolis is in danger!” Superman said as he and Lois zoomed out of the Fortress. “I have to stop Luthor!”

Luthor blew up a building
as Superman and Lois arrived.
“The buildings are all empty,”
Superman said.
“At least no one got hurt.”

“Metropolis is mine!”
said Luthor.
He blasted another building.

A piece of stone fell toward Lois.
Superman soared up to catch it
and then tossed it
safely away.

“I can destroy Luthor’s laser

with my heat vision,” Superman said.

Two red beams shot out of his eyes.

Luthor’s weapon blew up.

Superman stopped Luthor's evil plot.
"Your days of making threats
are over!" he told the villain.
Superman gave Luthor to the police.

“Thanks for the story, Superman,” Lois said when they returned to the Daily Planet.

“I can’t wait until Clark sees it!”

“Who’s Clark?” Superman asked.

“Never mind!” Lois said.

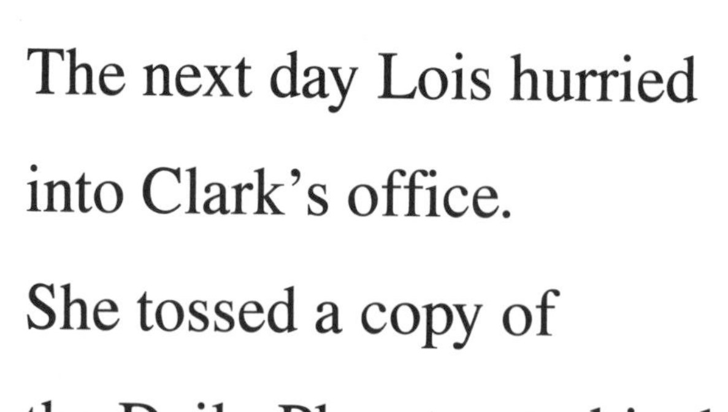

The next day Lois hurried
into Clark's office.
She tossed a copy of
the Daily Planet onto his desk.

"Here's what I was doing
while you were just sitting around,"
Lois said to Clark.
"How do you do it?" Clark asked.
"That's my secret!" said Lois.

Lois walked out of Clark's office.

Clark smiled to himself.

"I have a secret, too," he said.

"I am Superman!"